The CAPTAIN UNDERPANTS EXTRA-CRUNCHY BOOK O' FUN

BY DAV PILKEY

SCHOLASTIC

For Kathy and Anamika

Scholastic Children's Books,
Euston House, 24 Eversholt Street,
London NW1 1DB, UK
a division of Scholastic Ltd
London ~ New York ~ Toronto ~ Auckland ~
Mexico City ~ New Delhi ~ Hong Kong

First published in the US by Scholastic Inc., 2001
First published in the UK by Scholastic Ltd, 2001

10 digit ISBN 0 439 99344 X
13 digit ISBN 978 0439 99344 9

Printed in the UK by CPI Bookmarque, Croydon, CR0 4TD

15 17 19 20 18 16

Papers used by Scholastic Children's Books are made from wood
grown in sustainable forests.

GEORGE AND HAROLD'S COLLEGE O' ART

PAY ATTENTION NOW---This will be on The Test!

Hi everybody. It's Time To LEARN How To make Your Own comic Books!

IT's EASY--- And FUN!!!

ALL You NEED is some PAPER, Pencils, ERASERS And A STAPLER.

ERASER

MR. STAPLEY

FIRST You HAVE To Think up A STORY.

And The best WAY To do THAT is To CREATE CHARACTERS,

WE'LL USE CAPTAIN UNDERPANTS AS OUR GOOD GUY.

NOW WE HAVE TO THINK UP A BAD GUY.

HOW ABOUT A BIG, HAIRY TOILET WITH WEREWOLF FANGS?

HA-HA-OK!

NOW THAT WE'VE GOT OUR BAD GUY, WE NEED TO KNOW ALL ABOUT HIM... WHAT POWERS DOES HE HAVE? HOW DID HE BECOME SO EVIL?

LASER BEAM

KUNG-FU GRIP

P.U.

STINKY FEET

ATOMIC BUTT

NUCLEAR WASTE IS OFTEN TO BLAME FOR CREATING EVIL MONSTERS. IT'S THE COMIC BOOK MAKER'S BEST FRIEND!

NEW CLEAR WASTE

NOW WE NEED A STORY, SO LET YOUR IMAGINATION RUN WILD! THIS REQUIRES LOTS OF DAYDREAMING!

DAYDREAMING IS FUN, AND YOU CAN DO IT ALMOST ANYWHERE--IN CLASS, ON THE BUS, OR EVEN AT HOME!

DAYDREAMERS AT WORK! -DO NOT DISTURB!!

EDITOR'S NOTE: You really shouldn't daydream in class!

ANOTHER GREAT WAY TO THINK UP STORIES IS CALLED "BRAINSTORMING". THIS IS WHERE YOU GET TOGETHER WITH A FRIEND AND LET THE IDEAS FLY!

LET'S MAKE HIS ARMS AND LEGS REA... SO WHE... FALLS...

WE SHOULD MAKE IT LIKE THAT MOVIE ABOUT THE KILLER APE.

HIS LASER BEAMS SHOULD BE REALLY... SO WHEN CAPTAIN...

YOU MEAN "TITANIC?"

..BUT THAT WHAT ENDS

OH YEAH! WE CAN TELL THE T...

NO! THE ONE WITH THE BIG GORILLA!

"GONE WITH THE WIND?"

HA-HA-H HA-HA!!

HA-HA HA-HA!

THAT'S IT!

THEN YOU DRAW HIS FALLING!

THEN WE C... THE ENDING CHANGES T...

YEAH!

REMEMBER: TWO BRAINS ARE OFTEN BETTER THAN ONE!

When you've figured out your story, you can start drawing your comic. This is where TEAMWORK comes in handy. I do ALL The writing 'cause I'm A good speller...

...And I do ALL The drawing because I'm a good ARTist!

Don't worry if you make mistakes --- it happens to the best of us.

That's why They invented ERASERS.

RUB RUB RUB

Now just keep writing and drawing until you've finished Telling your story.

Many comic books end with a big fight. If you have trouble writing action scenes, you can always use Flip-O-Rama instead.

Turn to page 24 to learn how to make your very own FLIP-O-RAMAS.

When you're finally done, make a cover. Then staple all of your pages together.

TA-DAAA! Your very own comic book!

Now go make copies of it and sell them in the playground !!!

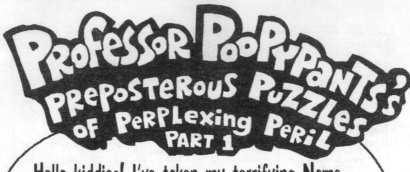

Professor PoopyPants's Preposterous Puzzles of Perplexing Peril
PART 1

Hello kiddies! I've taken my terrifying Name Change-O-Chart 2000 and turned it into a **WORD SEARCH PUZZLE!** Try to find all the names from the chart below in the puzzle on the right. Look up, down, across and backwards!

FIRST CHART: Use the First Letter of Your First Name To Determine Your **NEW** First Name!

A = Stinky
B = Lumpy
C = Buttercup
D = Gidget
E = Crusty
F = Greasy
G = Fluffy
H = Cheeseball
I = Chim-Chim

J = Poopsie
K = Flunky
L = Booger
M = Pinky
N = Zippy
O = Goober
P = Doofus
Q = Slimy

R = Loopy
S = Snotty
T = Falafel
U = Dorky
V = Squeezit
W = Oprah
X = Skipper
Y = Dinky
Z = Zsa-Zsa

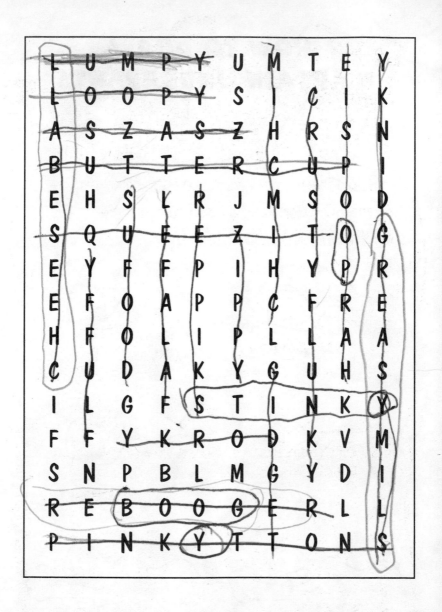

```
L U M P Y U M T E Y
L O O P Y S I C I K
A S Z A S Z H R S N
B U T T E R C U P D
E H S L R J M S O G
S Q U E E Z I T P R
E Y F F P I H Y R E
E Y F A P P C F A A
H F O L I P L L H S
C U D A K Y G U H Y
I L G F S T I N K Y
F F Y K R O D K V M
S N P B L M G Y D I
R E B O O G E R L L
P I N K Y T T O N S
```

(Answers on page 93)

HOW TO DRAW
CAPTAIN UNDERPANTS

1.

2.

3.

4.

5.

6.

7.

8.

9.

10.

11.

12.

13.

14.

15.

16.

13

CAN YOU ESCAPE DOCTOR NAPPY'S DEVASTATING NAPPY OF DOOM?

(Answer on page 93)

Now, pretend you're playing a fun game!

HA-HA-HA

HEY! WHAT'S GOING ON OVER THERE?!!?

CLINK

IT'S A FUN GAME. YOU TRY TO drop A PENNY OFF YOUR chin And cATCh it in The FUNNEL. IT'S Really hard!

Oh YEAh?!!? WELL LET ME TRY IT, bub!

OK!

When your victim leans back to put the penny on his chin...

...Pour your water into the funnel.

...Now RUN!

HA-HA-HA A-HA-HA-HA!

THE PERILOUS PUZZLE OF PROFESSOR POOPYPANTS

ACROSS

2. The alien spacemen were named Zorx, Klax, and Jennifer.

4. Harold's best friend is _____.

5. "George is the kid on the left with the _____ and the flat-top."

7. George's best friend is _____.

8. Don't get "weeded out" by the Deliriously Dangerous Death-Defying _____ of Doom.

10. Dr Nappy wanted to blow up the _____.

12. Captain Underpants is also known as a principal named Mr _____.

14. Don't get flushed by the Turbo _____ 2000!

15. "Yum, _____, eat 'em up!"

DOWN

1. "Never underestimate the power of _____."

3. _____ Horwitz Elementary School

4. Don't get blown up by the Goosy-grow 4000.

6. Ms Ribble is George and Harold's _____.

7. "Harold is the one on the right with the T-shirt and the bad _____."

9. Captain Underpants fights crime with Wedgie _____.

11. Professor Poopypants's first name.

13. Don't get shrunk by the Shrinky-_____ 2000.

(Answers on page 94)

HOW TO DRAW
THE TURBO TOILET 2000

1.

2.

3.

4.

5.

6.

7.

8.

PROFESSOR POOPYPANTS'S PREPOSTEROUS PUZZLES OF PERPLEXING PERIL PART 2

So you solved my last puzzle, eh? Well don't get too full of yourself. This puzzle is <u>much harder</u> – it's got DIAGONALS! Try to find all the names from the chart below in the puzzle on the right. Look up, down, across, <u>diagonally</u> and backwards!

2

SECOND CHART: USE the first Letter of your LAST NAME to determine the FIRST half of YOUR NEW Last Name.

A = ~~Diaper~~
B = ~~Toilet~~
C = Giggle
D = ~~Bubble~~
E = Girdle
F = Barf
G = ~~Lizard~~
H = ~~Waffle~~
I = Cootie

J = Monkey
K = Potty
L = Liver
M = ~~Banana~~
N = Rhino
O = Burger
P = Hamster
Q = Toad

R = Gizzard
S = ~~Pizza~~
T = Gerbil
U = ~~Chicken~~
V = Pickle
W = Chuckle
X = Tofu
Y = ~~Gorilla~~
Z = Stinker

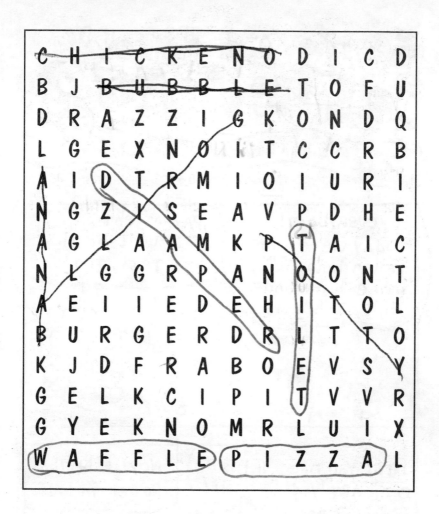

```
C H I C K E N O D I C D
B J B U B B L E T O F U
D R A Z Z I G K O N D Q
L G E X N O I T C C R B
A I D T R M I O I U R I
N G Z I S E A V P D H E
A G L A A M K P T A I C
N L G G R P A O O N T
A E I I E D E H I T O L
B U R G E R D R L T T O
K J D F R A B O E V S Y
G E L K C I P I T V V R
G Y E K N O M R L U I X
W A F F L E P I Z Z A L
```

(Answers on page 94)

George And Harold's College O' Art 2

MAKE YOUR OWN FLIP-O-RAMA!!!

Hi, everybody! Today we're gonna LEARN how To make homemade FLIP-O-RAMAS!

PAY ATTENTION... This will be on The TEST, TOO!

First You need An ordinary A4 Piece of PAPER.

Got it!

Now fold The Paper in hALf.

BECAUSE MOST PAPER IS A LITTLE TRANSPARENT, YOU SHOULD STILL KINDA BE ABLE TO SEE YOUR DRAWING UNDERNEATH.

I CAN KINDA SEE IT!

IF YOU CAN'T SEE YOUR DRAWING UNDERNEATH THE TOP SHEET OF PAPER, JUST HOLD IT UP TO A SUNNY WINDOW.

COOL!

NOW WE'RE GOING TO DO SOME TRACING ON THE TOP PAGE. THE **1ST** RULE IS:

IF YOU <u>DON'T</u> WANT SOMETHING TO MOVE, **TRACE IT!!!**

And since he's dribbling the ball on the floor, I'll re-draw the ball down on the floor.

HAROLD HAS just shown The **2ND** rule of Flip-o-Rama: If you want something to move, you must **RE-DRAW** it in a new position.

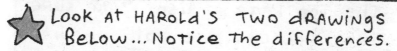

⭐ Look at HAROLD'S two drawings below... Notice the differences.

FIRST dRAWING (BOTTOM PAGE)

SECOND dRAWING (TOP PAGE)

You might need some Adjustments To make it work better.

I'm going to draw Action Lines on The Top page.

Like Any great ART, FLiP-O-RAMA takes Lots of PRactice.

But The more You PRactise, the better you'll get!

RUB RUB RUB RUB

Soon you cAn move on to more exciting FLip-O-RAMAS, Like Kicks, Punches And head injuries!

You'LL be A FLiP-O-RAMA MASTER, with The power to AmAze And delight everyone you meet.

...WeLL, ALmost everyone!

HAPPY FLiPPiNG

HEY KiDS--- Check out the WORLD'S EASIEST FLiP-O-RAMA!!!

☆ ☆ ☆ ☆ ☆ ☆
SPESHEL NOTES
FOR FLIP-O-RAMISTS

1. Typing paper and notebook paper work best.

2. Although you need to trace, don't use tracing paper. It will ruin the Affect.

3. Grown-ups will freak out if your flip-o-Ramas Feacher "people" beating each other up. To get around this, draw <u>robots</u> and <u>monsters</u> instead. (For Some REAson, Grown-ups think thats O.K. ...Go Figure!)

4. You can get good ideas by studying the FLIP-O-RamAS in the "CAptain underpants" and "Ricky Ricotta" Books.

"Knock knock?"
"Who's there?"
"I'm a pile-up."
"I'm a pile-up who?"
"No, you're not! Don't be so hard on yourself, buddy!"

Q) What did the mummy buffalo say to the baby buffalo when he went off to school?
A) Bison.

Q) What does lightning wear beneath its clothes?
A) Thunderwear.

Q) What should you do if you get swallowed by an elephant?
A) Jump up and down 'til you're all pooped out.

Q) Why did Batman cross his legs?
A) He had to go to the batroom.

Q) If you had fifty bananas in one hand, and twenty-five litres of ice cream in the other, what would you have?
A) Really big hands.

HOW TO DRAW
PROFESSOR POOPYPANTS

1.
2.
3.
4.

5.
6.
7.

8.
9.

10.

39

THE CAFETERIA LADIES' CRAZY CROSSWORD

ACROSS

3. Dr _____ was defeated soon after George shot fake doggy doo-doo at him.

5. *The Attack of the _____ Toilets.*

6. Watch out for the Equally Evil Lunchroom _____ Nerds.

8. Pippy P. Poopypants invented the _____ Jogger 2000.

10. "Hooray for Captain _____!"

11. Don't drink the Evil Zombie Nerd _____!

13. Captain Underpants often shouts "_____-La-Laaaaa!"

14. *Cheesy Animation Technology* is more commonly known as _____-O-Rama.

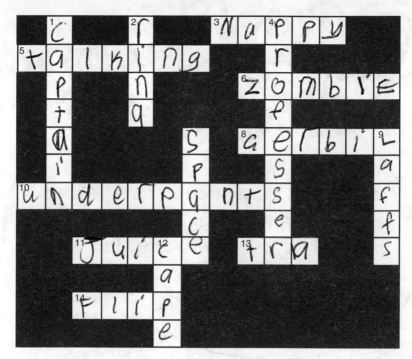

DOWN

1. *The Adventures of* _____ *Underpants.*
2. Mr Krupp was transformed into a superhero by the 3-D Hypno-_____.
4. *The Perilous Plot of* _____ *Poopypants.*
7. Zorx, Klax and Jennifer were evil guys from outer _____.
9. A popular way to misspell the word "laughs".
12. Captain Underpants wears a red _____.

(Answers on page 94)

Professor PoopyPants's Preposterous Puzzles of Perplexing Peril
PART 3

Now comes the hardest puzzle of all. If you mess this one up, you must use the three Name Change-O-Chart 2000 charts to change your name FOR EVER! Try to find all the names from the chart below in the puzzle on the right. Look up, down, across, <u>diagonally</u> and backwards!

3

Third Chart: Use the last letter of your last name to determine the second half of your NEW last name.

A = ~~Head~~
B = ~~Mouth~~
C = Face
D = Nose
E = Tush
F = Breath
G = Pants
H = Shorts
I = Lips

J = Honker
K = ~~Butt~~
L = ~~Brain~~
M = Tushie
N = Chunks
O = Hiney
P = Biscuits
Q = Toes

R = Buns
S = ~~Fanny~~
T = Sniffer
U = Sprinkles
V = Kisser
W = ~~Squirt~~
X = Humperdinck
Y = ~~Brains~~ Brain
Z = Juice

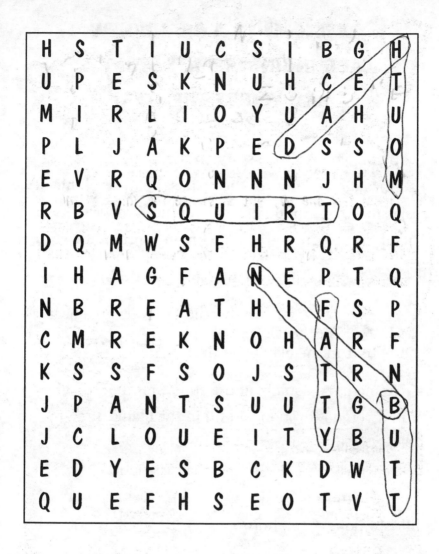

H	S	T	I	U	C	S	I	B	G	H
U	P	E	S	K	N	U	H	C	E	T
M	I	R	L	I	O	Y	U	A	H	U
P	L	J	A	K	P	E	D	S	S	O
E	V	R	Q	O	N	N	N	J	H	M
R	B	V	S	Q	U	I	R	T	O	Q
D	Q	M	W	S	F	H	R	Q	R	F
I	H	A	G	F	A	N	E	P	T	Q
N	B	R	E	A	T	H	I	F	S	P
C	M	R	E	K	N	O	H	A	R	F
K	S	S	F	S	O	J	S	T	R	N
J	P	A	N	T	S	U	U	T	G	B
J	C	L	O	U	E	I	T	Y	B	U
E	D	Y	E	S	B	C	K	D	W	T
Q	U	E	F	H	S	E	O	T	V	T

(Answers on page 95)

WELCOME TO A BRAND-NEW CAPTAIN UNDERPANTS STORY. . . AND YOU'RE THE STAR!

Before you read the story on the following pages, go through and find all the blanks. Below each blank is a small description of what you need to write in the blank. Just fill in the blank with an appropriate word.

For example, if the blank looks like this:

_____, you would think up an adjective
(an adjective)

and put it in the blank like this: ___**stinky**___.
(an adjective)

Remember, don't read the story first. It's more fun if you go through and fill in the blanks first, THEN read the story.

When you're done, follow the instructions at the bottom of each page to complete the illustrations. Cool, huh?

JUST FOR REMINDERS:
a **Verb** is an <u>action</u> word (like jump, swim, kick, squish, run, etc.)
an **Adjective** is a word that <u>describes</u> a person, place or thing (lumpy, dumb, purple, hairy, etc.)

CAPTAIN UNDERPANTS VS THE EVIL MONSTER
(STARRING GEORGE, HAROLD AND YOU!)

Once upon a time, George, Harold and their

friend, __Grace__ , were busy studying
(your name)

about the wonders of __Stinky__
(an adjective)

__Poo__ , when their new science
(disgusting things)

teacher, Mr __marfart__ , accidentally
(a funny name)

spilled some __Poo__ __liquid__
(a gross adjective)   (a liquid)

on a pile of toxic __Ailiens__ .
(silly things)

(Draw yourself
sitting here)

(Draw the teacher spilling
liquid on to some toxic stuff)

Suddenly, the pile began to morph into

a giant, evil ___Poo monster___.
(a silly thing)

"Help," cried ___Dedan___, "a
(somebody in your class)

giant, evil ___Poo monster___
(the silly thing you just used above)

just stepped on my lunchbox and ate up

___Mr Chicken!___"
(your gym teacher's name)

"Oh NO!" cried Mr Krupp. "The poor

lunchbox!"

↑
(Draw the giant,
evil monster)

↖
(Draw the kid
in your class)

George, Harold and _____<u>grac</u>_____
(your name)

tried to escape by hiding behind a

_____<u>chair</u>_____. Then _____<u>grace</u>_____
(a very small thing)   (your name)

snapped _____<u>her</u>_____ fingers.
(either "his" or "her")

Soon, a _____<u>calosle</u>_____ grin came
(an adjective)

across Mr Krupp's face as he dropped

his _____<u>Too big</u>_____ <u>trouserson the flod</u>
(an adjective)   (an article of clothing)

and ran to his office.

(Draw yourself)   (Draw the thing you're all hiding behind)   (Draw the giant, evil monster)

Soon, Captain Underpants

_____sleeped_____ through the

wall. He grabbed a _____teeny_____
(an adjective)

_____marbel_____ and hit the monster
(a thing)

on its _____head_____.
(a body part)

"Ouchies!" screamed the monster. It

turned and _____stomped_____
(a fight move ending in "ed")

Captain Underpants on his

_____toe_____.
(a body part)

(Draw
yourself)

(Draw the monster fighting
Captain Underpants)

Grace quickly mixed up a bottle
(your name)

of _Milk_ with a jar of toxic,
(something a kid would drink)

green _snot_ .
(an adjective)   (disgusting things)

"Hey, _grace_ ," said George,
(your name)

"where'd you find that jar of crazy stuff?!!?"

"It was right here next to this barrel of

toxic _slimy_ _poo poo_ ,"
(an adjective)   (different disgusting things)

said _grace_ .
(your name)

"Oh," said Harold. "That makes sense."

(Draw yourself creating
a strange mixture)

(Draw the contents of the barrel
coming out the top)

BARREL OF

_____Grace_____ shook up the strange
(your name)

mixture and threw it at the monster.

" _Abracadadah_ " screamed
(something you might scream or cheer)

the monster as it fell over and died of a

massive _____leg_____ attack.
(a body part)

"That makes sense, too," said George.

Unfortunately, some of the mixture

splashed on Captain Underpants's head,

and he turned back into Mr Krupp.

(Draw yourself throwing the strange   (Draw the monster
concoction on to the monster)   getting splashed)

"HOLY _CRAZY_ _DONKEY_!"
(an adjective)   (silly animals)

shouted Mr Krupp. "I'll bet that George,

Harold and _Grace_ are responsible
(your name)

for this mess!" So he punished the three kids

by making them _kick_ in the
(an action verb)

classroom for _200_ hours.
(a room in the school)   (a number)

"This has got to be the dumbest story

we've ever been in," said George.

"Don't blame me," said Harold. "_Grace_
(your name)

wrote it!"

↑
(Draw yourself
looking guilty)

ZORX, KLAX AND Jennifer's Big, BAD BATCH OF ZOMBIE NERD Juice

(Answer on page 95)

FINAL EXAM

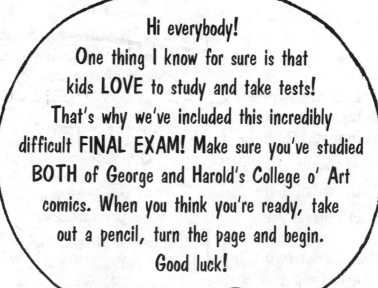

Hi everybody!
One thing I know for sure is that
kids **LOVE** to study and take tests!
That's why we've included this incredibly
difficult **FINAL EXAM!** Make sure you've studied
BOTH of George and Harold's College o' Art
comics. When you think you're ready, take
out a pencil, turn the page and begin.
Good luck!

1. What's the BEST way to think up a story?

a) create characters

b) put a grilled cheese sandwich on your head

c) roll around in steak sauce, then bark like a dog

2. What is often to blame for creating monsters?

a) society

b) school dinners

c) nuclear waste

3. What two things also help you think up stories?

a) brainstorming and daydreaming

b) braindreaming and daystorming

c) daybraining and dreamstorming

4. Don't worry about making mistakes. That's why they invented _____.

a) lawyers

b) erasers

c) soap-on-a-rope

5. If you have trouble writing action scenes, you can always use _____.

a) a ghost writer

b) Flip-O-Rama

c) egg-salad

6. When making comics, be prepared to:

a) win friends and influence people

b) smell like cheese puffs

c) suffer for your art

7. What's the world's EASIEST Flip-O-Rama?

a) a guy with a chicken up his nose

b) a guy with a basketball ✓

c) a guy with a basketball up his nose

8. The FIRST rule of Flip-O-Rama is: If you don't want something to move, _____.

a) trace it ✓

b) put it in a "time-out"

c) threaten to stop the car

9. The SECOND rule of Flip-O-Rama is: If you want something to move, you must _____.

a) make rude noises with your armpits

b) drink lots of prune juice

c) re-draw it in a new position

10. The more you practise, _____.

a) the better you get ✓

b) the dumber you get

c) the stinkier you get

Now put your pencil down, and let's see how you did.

If you got at least 6 right, CONGRATULATIONS! You've just graduated from George and Harold's College o' Art.

Write to us now, and we'll send you your "P.H.D." (Pilkey Honorary Diploma), a make-it-yourself graduation cap with real artificial tassels, and a membership card. Plus, you'll have the honour of being able to write "P.H.D." after your name from now on. Lots of people have to go to real colleges, study for years, and pay thousands of pounds for that honour. But if you act now, it can all be yours absolutely FREE!

Just send a self-addressed, stamped, A4 envelope to:

YOUR NAME
And Address

"Me WAhT MY P.H.D."
c/o Scholastic
Commonwealth House
1-19 New Oxford Street
London WC1A 1NU

Q) Why do sharks live in salt water?
A) Because pepper water makes them sneeze.

Q) How do you make a tissue dance?
A) Put a little boogie into it.

Q) Why did Tigger stick his head in the toilet?
A) He was looking for "Pooh".

Q) Who is Peter Pan's worst-smelling friend?
A) Stinkerbell.

Q) What nationality are you when you go to the bathroom?
A) European.

A woman walks into a pet store and says, "Can I get a puppy for my daughter?"

"Sorry, lady," says the pet store owner. "We don't do swaps."

Hairy Potty

AND the

UNDERWEAR of JUSTISE

BY G. R. BEARD and H.M. HUtchins

Onse upon a time There was a scientist who worked At "Hair GROup for Guys."

HAIR GROUP LaBRATO

He was trying To invent a Hair Growth Formyula.

Hmmm.

But it didn't work.

Fooey!

Then he tried Adding **NEWCLEAR WASTE** To his concockshon.

NEW CLEARE WASTE

The scientist decided to get Rid of The bad Formyula so that nothing else would grow big and hairy and evil.

So he pored it down the toilet.

BUT---He forgot to Flush!

Soon, the Toilet grew hair.

Then the Toilet grew Big.

Then The Toilet grew evil

The scientist Reached FOR A can of "POTTY-BE-GONE" Brand® Toilet Remover...

Hairy Potty shot his
Lazer And made A Hole
in The WALL.

ZAP

I'm FRee!!!

Then He RAN AROUND CAUSING MISCHiFF.

BOB'S DINER
AT BOB'S DINER, YOU'LL' Find That
We Pick THE BEST inGredyents.
YOUR NOSE **KNOWS** The diFReNSe!

Hmmm.

ZAP

BOB'S
AT BOB'S DINER,
We Pick
YOUR NOSE

HAW
HAW
HAW

Then Hairy Potty
RAN To A School.

LA-LA
LA-LA

HAIRY POTTY chased OUR HERO outside.

HEYMON'S GIFTS

Who makes the CUTEST GIFTS And the Most delishous cheese? ...WE DO!

ZAP

HEY Who CUT the Cheese?

CAPTAIN UNDERPANTS WAS FASTER THAN A speeding waistband...

zip

ZAP!

... MORE POWER-FULL THAN BOXER SHORTS...

TRIP

... And Abel to leap TALL Bildings without getting a wedgie.

TRA-LA LAAAAA

ZAP

BONK

BUT HAIRY Potty WAS Powerful, too. He shot A EvIL Lazer Beam at Captain Underpants.

ZAAP

Hey! what's going On here? How come your not dead?

NEVER UNDER-ESTIMATE THE Power of UNDERWEAR!

Finally, Captain Underpants and Hairy Potty got into a big, terible fight.

ROAR

TRA-LA-LAAAAA!

WARNING

The following fight contains very graphic violins.

Please cover your eyes when you turn the pages or you might get emoshinally Disterbed.

—Thank You

FLiP-O-RAMA

HERE's HOW it WORKS !!!!

STEP 1
Plase your Left Hand inside the doted Lines marked "LEFT HAND HERE" Hold the BOOK open FLAT

STEP 2
GRASP the Right-hand page with your Right Thumb and index Finger (inside the doted Lines MARKED "RiGHT THUMB HERE").

STEP 3
Now Quickly FLiP THE Right-hand page back and FOURTH UNTIL the piTCHER apears to be animated.

(FOR extrA fun, tRy adding your own Sound-AFFECKS!)

FLIP-O-RAMA #1

(pages 71 and 73)

Remember, flip only page 71
while you are fliping, be sure
you can see the pitcher on
page 71   And the one on
page 73 .

If you flip Quickly,
the two pitchers will
start to look like
one Animated pitcher.

Left Hand
Here

The Eyeball Basher

RIGHT
Thume
Here

The EyeBall Basher

FLIP-O-RAMA #2

(pages 75 and 77)

Remember, flip only page 75 while you are fliping, be sure you can see the pitcher on page 75 And the one on Page 77 .

If you flip Quickly, the two pitchers will Start to Look Like One Animated pitcher.

Left Hand Here

THE KOO-KOO CLAP

Right
Thume
Here

THE KOO-KOO CLAP

FLIP-O-RAMA #3

(pages 79 and 81)

Remember, flip _only_ page 79 while you are fliping, be sure you can see the pitcher on page 79 _And_ the one on page 81.

If you flip Quickly, the two pitchers will Start to look like _One_ Animated pitcher.

Left Hand Here

The Potty Pounder

Right
Thume
Here

The Potty Pounder

FLIP-O-RAMA #4

(pages 83 and 85)

Remember, flip only page 83
while you are fliping, be sure
you can see the pitcher on
page 83 And the one on
page 85.

If you flip Quickly,
the two pitchers will
start to look like
One Animated pitcher.

Left Hand
Here

The Psycko Stomp

Right Thume Here

84

The Psycko Stomp

ANSWERS

Word Search
p. 11

Maze
p. 14

93

Crossword
p. 19

Word Search
p. 23

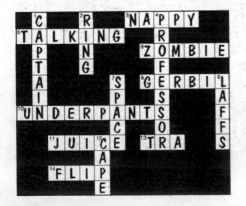

Crossword
p. 41

Word Search
p. 43

Maze
p. 52